Dear Parent:
Your child's love of reading starts here!

Every child learns to read in a different way and at his or her own speed. Some go back and forth between reading levels and read favorite books again and again. Others read through each level in order. You can help your young reader improve and become more confident by encouraging his or her own interests and abilities. From books your child reads with you to the first books he or she reads alone, there are I Can Read Books for every stage of reading:

SHARED READING
Basic language, word repetition, and whimsical illustrations, ideal for sharing with your emergent reader

BEGINNING READING
Short sentences, familiar words, and simple concepts for children eager to read on their own

READING WITH HELP
Engaging stories, longer sentences, and language play for developing readers

READING ALONE
Complex plots, challenging vocabulary, and high-interest topics for the independent reader

I Can Read Books have introduced children to the joy of reading since 1957. Featuring award-winning authors and illustrators and a fabulous cast of beloved characters, I Can Read Books set the standard for beginning readers.

A lifetime of discovery begins with the magical words "I Can Read!"

Visit www.icanread.com for information
on enriching your child's reading experience.

For Susie and Don
—T.B.

I Can Read® and I Can Read Book® are trademarks of HarperCollins Publishers.

Little Penguin and the Mysterious Object
Copyright © 2020 by Tadgh Bentley
All rights reserved. Printed in the United States of America.
No part of this book may be used or reproduced in any manner whatsoever without written permission except in the case of brief quotations embodied in critical articles and reviews. For information address HarperCollins Children's Books, a division of HarperCollins Publishers, 195 Broadway, New York, NY 10007.
www.icanread.com

ISBN 978-0-06-269998-5 (trade bdg.) — ISBN 978-0-06-269997-8 (pbk.)

Book design by Andrea Vandergrift
20 21 22 23 24 LSCC 10 9 8 7 6 5 4 3 2 1 ❖ First Edition

I Can Read!

BEGINNING READING 1

Little Penguin
and the Mysterious Object

Story by Laura Driscoll
Pictures by Tadgh Bentley

BALZER + BRAY
An Imprint of HarperCollinsPublishers

Oh! You made it!

Thank goodness!

We found a . . . thing.

And we don't know

what to do with it.

Look at this!

We found it here

this morning.

What could it be?

Do you know?

It is big.

It is heavy.

It is hard to tell

which way is up.

It is . . . not tasty.

And it is not at all comfy
to sit on.

We have never seen anything like it.

Where did it come from?

Is there someone,

somewhere,

who needs it back?

And what is it for?

We all want to know.

After all . . .

Penguins
Love a Mystery!

Franklin has an idea.

"I think it is a back scratcher,"

he says.

What do you think?

"No, look!" says Reginald.

He spins the spinny part.

Whoosh!

"It must be a feather dryer!"

he says.

Could that be it?

My tummy rumbles.

It makes me think of chili.

And that gives me an idea.

"Could it be the world's largest
chili mixer?" I say.
Oh, I really hope so.

Other penguins jump on

and use it as an exercise machine.

Not as much fun as my idea,

I would say.

But it works.

Or does it work better

as a kickball launcher?

Penguins love kickball.

But this is not kickball.

This is . . .

spinball!

Oh no!

The ball is stuck in the snow.

"I can help!" I say.

"I can reach the ball using this . . .

ladder?"

Ta-da!

Uh-oh.

Yikes!

Oh, help!

Look out!

Coming through!

I don't think this whatever-it-is
is supposed to work this way!

Splash!

I hope it is waterproof.

Of course!

Now I know what this is.

Why didn't you tell me?

It is a boat.

Um.
I mean,
a *submarine*!